THIS
BOOK
WAS
DONATED
BY

Dr. Milz

The Stone Dancers

BY NORA MARTIN

ILLUSTRATED BY JILL KASTNER

ATHENEUM BOOKS FOR YOUNG READERS

ATHENEUM BOOKS FOR YOUNG READERS
An imprint of Simon & Schuster Children's Publishing Division
1230 Avenue of the Americas, New York, New York 10020
Text copyright © 1995 by Nora Martin
Illustrations copyright © 1995 by Jill Kastner
All rights reserved including the right of reproduction
in whole or in part in any form.
Book design by Julie Y. Quan
The text for this book is set in Berkeley Old Style Medium.
The illustrations are rendered in oil paint.
Manufactured in China
First edition
10 9 8 7 6 5 4 3 2 1

LIBRARY OF CONGRESS CATALOGING-IN-PUBLICATION DATA
Martin, Nora B.
The stone dancers / by Nora Martin ; illustrated by Jill Kastner.
—1st ed.
p.   cm.
Summary: A young girl uses an old legend about stone dancers to
teach her mountain village a lesson in hospitality and sharing.
ISBN 0-689-80312-5
[1. Conduct of life—Fiction.   2. Mountain life—Fiction.]
I. Kastner, Jill, ill.   II. Title.
PZ7.M36416St   1995
[Fic]—dc20   94-18505

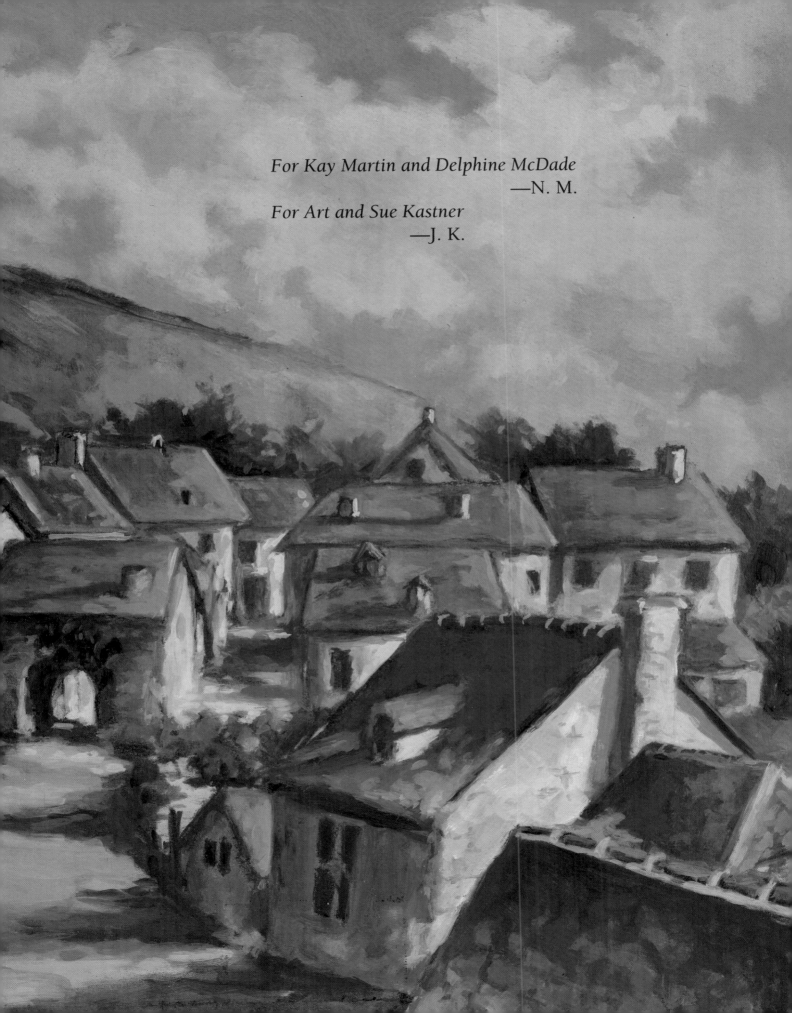

For Kay Martin and Delphine McDade
—N. M.

For Art and Sue Kastner
—J. K.

$\mathcal{H}$igh on a mountain near where the wind and the stars collide lie the ruins of an ancient castle, left long ago to crumble away stone by stone. From the base of the old castle walls, a narrow road winds down to the valley, and along this road are the few stone houses of a tiny village.

In one of these houses a young girl named Anise lives with her parents, her grandparents, and her brother, Donne. All year they work hard tending their goats and planting their fields.

But on dark winter nights, when the chores are finished, Grandpapa Besot sits on an old bench in front of the fire.

He gathers the children in close to his large, square body and tells them stories. Anise's favorite story is of their village long ago and of the marvelous castle that once towered above it.

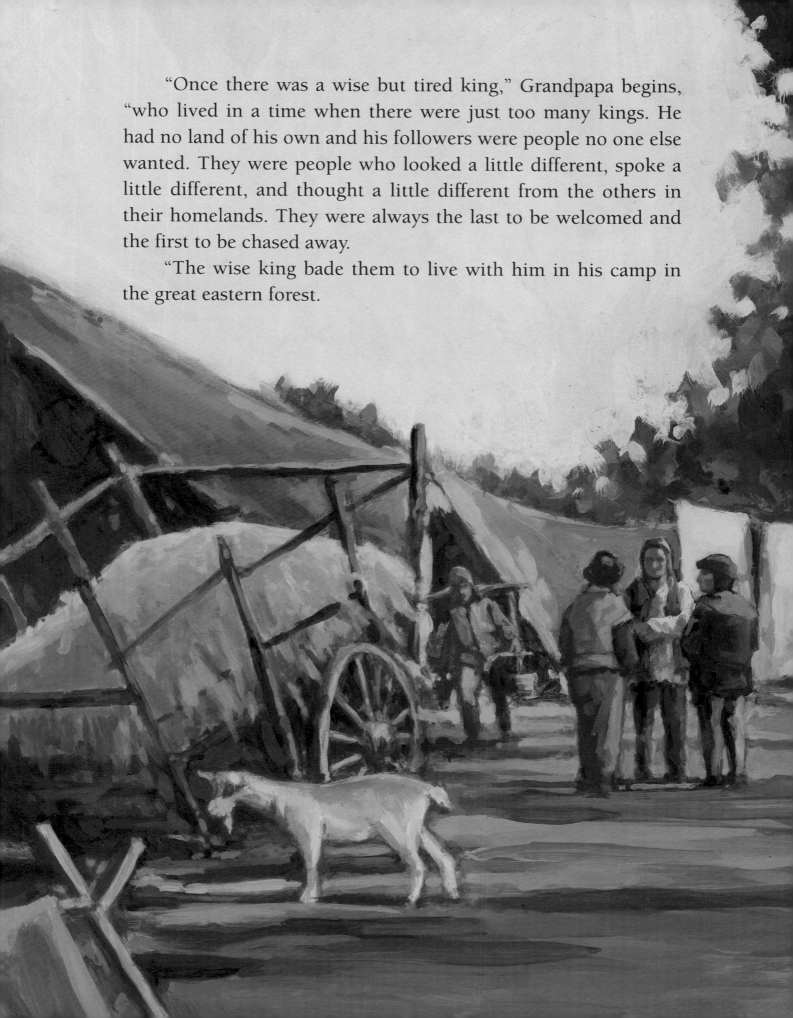

"Once there was a wise but tired king," Grandpapa begins, "who lived in a time when there were just too many kings. He had no land of his own and his followers were people no one else wanted. They were people who looked a little different, spoke a little different, and thought a little different from the others in their homelands. They were always the last to be welcomed and the first to be chased away.

"The wise king bade them to live with him in his camp in the great eastern forest.

"Their numbers grew, and soon they were so many that they began to attract the unfriendly attention of the kingdoms around them.

"The wise king told his followers, 'These other kings and their armies come like a great river. They seem to have many reasons to attack us. But I can think of none.'

"So the king and his subjects left the forest. They traveled south and west until they came to a range of dry mountains. They led their oxen up the side of the largest mountain until they could go no higher.

"There, under the king's directions, they built a stone castle rising into the sky. The king told his people, 'Here we will be safe.'

"The people danced in joy along the walls of their castle. They danced so all those like themselves could see them and know they would be welcomed into the wise king's new land.

"But the only people who saw the castle dwellers dancing were a few wandering shepherds who could not see clearly over the great distance. They mistook the king's followers for the stones of the mountain itself come to life. The herdsmen fled back to their villages with mysterious tales of dancers made of stone.

"With the passage of time, the castle people forgot their fears and moved into houses they built along the winding road. They became farmers and shepherds. Many people believe, children, that we are the descendants of that wise king and his followers."

Grandpapa gives both Anise and Donne a hug and a wink. "I have also heard it said that those who carry true goodness within them can sometimes see the stones on the ridge top come to life and take the form of the old king and his subjects."

"You silly old man," Grandmaman Besot scolds. "Do not fill these children's heads with such wastefulness. These are the imaginings of herdsmen and vagabonds who have nothing better to do with their time."

But Anise believes her Grandpapa's stories because at night, from her vine-framed window, she lifts her face skyward and sees beyond the shadows of the cliffs to where piles of stone that were once castle walls touch the misty air.

As the moonlight shines between the clouds, she can see the stones unfurl long, heavy arms as softly as a deep sigh. They rise on great stone legs and lift blank stone faces set on chiseled necks into the celestial light. Their boulder chests expand as they breathe in life. And after looking to one another as if in greeting, the huge bodies begin to dance.

The dancers move with the rhythm of the wind. On quiet summer nights they dance a caressing whisper dance, their long legs reaching in perfect honey slowness. In the howling storms

of winter, the dancers move with huge bursts of hard rock muscles, leaping and turning, lifting one another against the flashing sky. Their great weight crashes like thunder, shaking the mountain each time their feet strike the ground.

Anise watches for as long as she can, until at some time during the dance the light fades or the shadows lengthen and the dancers slip away into the distance of dreams. The next thing Anise knows, her mother's voice is calling up the stone steps for

One day as the villagers return from their fields, they see a wagon approach on the gravel-strewn road. Everyone stops to stare. Who could possibly be coming?

When the cart halts near the village fountain, the people see that it carries a man and a woman, with three children. They look tired and are covered in dirt. Anise watches the children hungrily eye the loaves of bread she carries.

The man in the cart addresses the crowd.

"I am René," he says. "And this is my family. We have come from far away in search of a home where we can live in peace. From across your valley we saw this mountain. We felt it calling to us, beckoning us, after we had given up all hope of finding refuge.

"Good people, would you let us make our home among you and plant an orchard between your fields and the roots of the mountain?"

The people of the village stare at the strangers in astonishment and begin to whisper to one another.

"You can see that they must come from some distant land. They look nothing like us."

"See how dirty those children are."

"Can you imagine? They think mountains call out to people!"

"Perhaps they are insane."

"They could be dangerous."

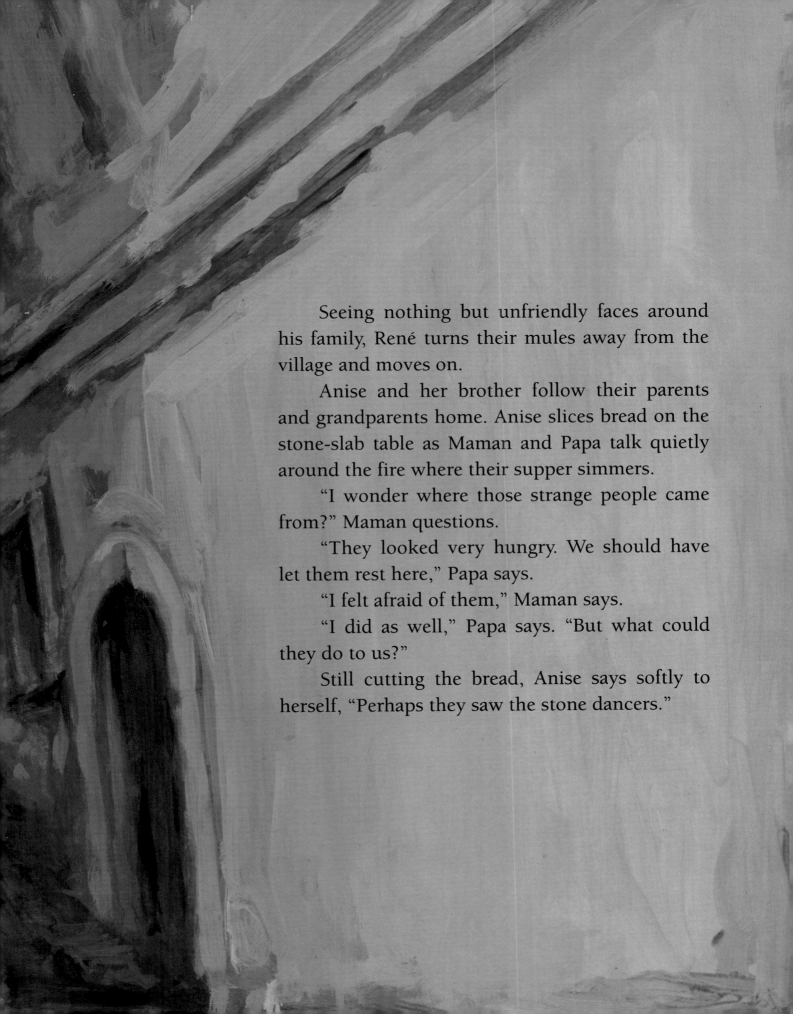

Seeing nothing but unfriendly faces around his family, René turns their mules away from the village and moves on.

Anise and her brother follow their parents and grandparents home. Anise slices bread on the stone-slab table as Maman and Papa talk quietly around the fire where their supper simmers.

"I wonder where those strange people came from?" Maman questions.

"They looked very hungry. We should have let them rest here," Papa says.

"I felt afraid of them," Maman says.

"I did as well," Papa says. "But what could they do to us?"

Still cutting the bread, Anise says softly to herself, "Perhaps they saw the stone dancers."

Maman and Papa look at each other. Without eating his supper, Papa puts on his black felt hat and leaves the house. He goes to each house of the village in the dusky light, knocking at every door, talking quietly with every neighbor. Late in the night, from where she sits in the window watching the ruins on the ridge, Anise sees his dark shape returning.

The next morning Maman calls Anise and Donne to break-fast very early.

"Come, children, quickly. Everyone must help," she says. "We are going in search of the family who came to us last evening. We will bring them back to live with us here in our village."

"But they are strangers," Donne says.

"They are only strangers until they live here and then they are our neighbors. And we must always care for our neighbors," Maman tells them.

As the new family is led back up the mountain into the village, they are surrounded by triumphant, noisy cheering.

"Welcome, welcome," the villagers shout.

Every household brings out food to be shared in a great feast around the fountain. Monsieur Jenet plays his violin and Anise dances with the other children to his lively tunes.

In the middle of the eating, the music, and the laughter, Paul, the eldest son of the new family, suddenly exclaims, "Look! Up there on the ridge top, something is moving."

Everyone stops and looks skyward, squinting their eyes, shading their brows with cupped hands.

"Oh, it is only the shadows of those little clouds reflecting against the stones," Grandmaman Besot says.

The music and happy chatter begin again. But Anise continues to watch the cliff top. She lets the breeze keep time as her mind dances joyfully with the stones upon the mountain ridge.